Snōshoo

~ The Stowaway Bunny ~

Written by
Alice Schellhorn Magrane
Illustrations by Brenda Brown

For Jack and Ric

Who always seem to enjoy my whimsical stories.

Much love and thanks for your encouragement.

ISBN: 1460969782
ISBN 13: 9781460969786
LCCN: 2011903672

stowaway /stow" a* way'/, noun

Definition:

1. Someone who hides aboard a ship, plane, boat or other vehicle (for example, Santa's sleigh) in order to travel without being seen.

On a sunny and cold Arctic morning,

(That's near the North Pole, you know.)

A play group of happy young bunnies,

Were enjoying a day in the snow.

1

These cute little bunnies have very thick fur
(It's white to blend in with the snow.)

Their back feet are large, which helps them run fast,

When there's somewhere that they need to go!

As they played in the sun, a new
bunny arrived,

And the others just stared with wide
eyes—

'Cause this little fellow—
he was sort of like them,

But his feet were a much different size!

His feet were like snowshoes—they really were huge!

And the others just laughed at him so;

Those feet let him run right on top of the snow,

As far from them as he could go!

4

When he finally stopped and looked all around,

The bunny got quite a surprise;
In the distance a building said "Santa's Workshop"

He couldn't believe his own eyes!

As he stared at the workshop he heard something move,

And he looked around trembling with fear; But the reindeer he saw was smiling and friendly—

He decided to let him come near.

The reindeer was Dasher who calmly explained,

As the bunny's eyes opened so wide;

That in Santa's Workshop the elves were near finished,

And Santa was ready to ride!

"Do you mean that he travels all over the world,

And brings toys in that sleigh over there?"

Dasher answered, "It's magic, and Santa

Brings presents to children who live everywhere!"

"I'd better go now.
It's almost that time."

Dasher ran towards The Workshop and sleigh;

The bunny stood still, then he quietly followed,

Not giving himself away.

As the reindeer were hitched to the sleigh and the elves brought the magical bag with the toys;

The bunny just waited, and at the right moment,

Jumped into it, making no noise!

"I'll see what this magical night is about,"
Said the bunny as he tried to hide;

"No one will know that I'm part of this show"…

And Santa began his long ride!

Santa went 'round the world as he always
has done,

Over rooftops he flew high and fast;
Leaving wonderful presents for good boys
and girls,

'Til his bag it was empty at last!

As they neared the North Pole at the
end of the night,

And came to the very last mile;
Santa pulled out the bunny—"Who is
this?" he asked,

As he chuckled and wore a big smile!

The bunny just trembled and tried to tell Santa…

He wanted to be a small part;
Of the magic of Christmas, but all he could hear

Was the thumping of his little heart!

Santa smiled at the bunny and with his deep voice said

"We'll have to call you Snōshoo.

With big feet like yours, you'll go where elves can't

On top of the snow when it's new!"

"You see there's a path that our elves must walk down to travel from workshop to barn;

And sometimes they sink into snowdrifts so deep,

That I worry they'll do themselves harm!"

Now Snōshoo the Stowaway
Bunny helps the elves when the
snow falls too deep;

He brings them the parts to make
all the toys,

All thanks to his very big feet!

Snōshoo the Stowaway Bunny hid away in
that magical sleigh;

What a wonderful ride;
Now he's helping, with pride,

To make toys for you on
Christmas Day!

18

Made in the USA
Coppell, TX
04 November 2019